J.R. SERRANO

Two Runaways

Two Runaways

by Jerry B. Jenkins

cover by Lou Specker

illustrated by Richard Wahl

STANDARD PUBLISHING
Cincinnati, Ohio 2942

Library of Congress Cataloging in Publication Data

Jenkins, Jerry B.
    Two runaways.

    (The Bradford family adventures; 2)
    Summary: When it seems everyone believes Daniel guilty of
cheating, he runs away with his friend Yolanda leaving behind a
frantic search.
    [1. Runaways—Fiction] I. Wahl, Richard, 1939-   ill.
II. Title. III. Series: Jenkins, Jerry B.   Bradford
family adventures; no. 2.
PZ7.J4138Tw 1984   [Fic]   83-24182
ISBN 0-87239-792-0

Dedication

To my nephew, Derek Jordan,
already a trooper

Contents

1

The Escape

It was two o'clock in the morning, but Daniel Bradford had not been asleep. He had stayed near his bedroom door, which was open about an inch, until after eleven when his parents came up to bed.

Then he had quickly, but silently, rushed to his bed where he pretended to be asleep. When they looked in on him, he heard his father say, "He'll still be in bed when I leave in the morning. But I think he'll be all right." He kissed Daniel on the cheek.

All right? Daniel thought. *I might never be all right again.* His mother said nothing as they left and closed his door.

When he thought it was safe, Daniel crept out of bed again and opened his door a little. He settled onto the floor with a blanket and listened to his parents talk.

He couldn't make out any of the words, but he knew they were talking about him, worrying about him, wondering if his dad should go to the Florida space center when Daniel was being bad.

Only I'm not being bad! Daniel reminded himself. *If only I could make them believe me!*

He had decided not to make his move until two hours after their light went out, and they quit talking. He wondered if Yolanda was still awake. *How could she sleep on a night like this?*

With the help of a tiny night light, Daniel quietly changed from his pajamas to a heavy, hooded, red sweatshirt, light blue jeans, white sports socks, and his new running shoes with the thick, bouncy soles.

He couldn't decide whether to take his jacket. It would be noisy, the arms rubbing against the sides when he walked. He tugged at his window and, when it opened just a crack, a bone-chilling gust of air made him shiver. You could never trust October.

He got the jacket from the closet, and also pulled down a small fabric bag, the one he used when he and his dad and big brother Jim went to play racquetball.

He stuffed it with three more pairs of jeans, a bunch of socks, underwear, and shirts. As he zipped it up, he got a sinking feeling in the pit of his stomach — the one he got when he thought of why he was leaving.

Yolanda's the only one who believes me, he thought. *But I know Grandpa will, too. He trusts me.*

Daniel dug in the bottom drawer of his dresser and pulled out eighty one-dollar bills. He'd saved them from his allowance over nearly two years. He folded them neatly and stuffed them deep into an inside pocket of his jacket.

He heard the furnace go on. While he would soon be too warm with his outdoor clothes on, he knew now was the best time to sneak down the hall, past his parents', his brother's, his sister's rooms, to the end of the hall where his dad's den used to be.

It was now the bedroom of his newly adopted sister, ten-year-old Yo-Yo. She had gotten her nickname, Yo-Yo, from her friends at the chilren's home. They had used just the first part of her first name and the last part of her last name, Yolanda Treviño.

Now the beautiful little Mexican girl with the gleaming smile was Yolanda Bradford, but she still liked it when Daniel called her Yo-Yo.

He put on his jacket and left his bag just outside his door. He tiptoed down the dark, carpeted hallway, holding his breath. His heart pounded so hard in his chest that he thought it would wake up everyone in the house.

He didn't want to knock on Yo-Yo's door, so he just pushed it open lightly with one hand. "Yo-Yo," he whispered. There was no answer. Daniel squinted into the darkness, trying to see if she was still in bed.

As he moved into the room, his knee hit the side of her bed, and Yolanda stirred. "Daniel?" she said.

"Shh," he said. "C'mon! Aren't you ready?"

"Are we really going?" she asked, propping herself up on one elbow.

"Of course!" he whispered. "Now come on!"

She got up and padded over to her dresser. "Wait in the hall," she said. He made a face and went out. A few minutes later she emerged, dressed pretty much the same way Daniel was and carrying a similar bag.

"We'd better get our toothbrushes, right Daniel?" she said. He shook his head and followed her to the bathroom. They groped in the darkness for their brushes and toothpaste and pushed them down into their bags.

They bumped into each other lightly on their

14

way down the stairs and their jackets made a squeaky noise. Yolanda giggled, but Daniel scowled.

They had to be very careful walking through the kitchen, because the floor was tile, not carpet. There was enough light so they didn't trip over anything, but it took Daniel a long time to silently open the door that led into the garage.

He couldn't shut it all the way because that would have made too much noise. He just pulled it to as far as he dared. "Are you sure you want to do this?" Yolanda asked. "Mom and Dad are going to be worried."

"Don't chicken out on me now, Yo-Yo," he said quickly.

"I'm not! But it took me long enough to get into a family. Why should I run away from the one I've got?"

He didn't answer. He just slipped their bags over the handlebars of his bike and lugged it to the side door. The big overhead door would have awakened everyone, so he edged the bike through the side door to the backyard. Yolanda followed him and shut the door.

Daniel gave her a dirty look for having made so much noise, but she couldn't see him in the dark. She started to climb onto the crossbars of his bike, but he whispered angrily, "Not yet,

"Hang on!"

Yo-Yo! Wait till we're on the other side of road!"

That made her cry, and they both felt bad.

Daniel thought he heard movement from within the house. He peered up through the back windows but saw nothing. Then he started Yolanda in the right direction by tugging at her sleeve.

She followed him around the house, staying in the shadows away from the floodlights. When they reached the road, Daniel looked in both directions. Then he jogged with his bike to the other side, with Yo-Yo right behind him.

He held the bike in place while she hopped into place. As he was mounting the bike, she said, "I didn't even get a chance to say good-bye to Jim and Maryann."

Daniel didn't say anything, for he didn't feel too good about that part. But his big brother and sister didn't believe him either. He pedaled slowly and wobbly a half mile down the country road to the six-lane highway. Daniel didn't expect to see any traffic, but far down the highway he saw headlights coming from the other direction.

He watched them carefully as they passed on the other side across the median. "Watch behind us, Yo-Yo," he said. "See if you can tell if that's a police car."

"It is!" she yelled, "and he's turning around!"

Daniel looked back, almost falling. She was right. The state trooper must have seen them. As the squad car wheeled through an emergency turnaround, it's spotlight licked across the highway to the shoulder.

"Hang on!" Daniel yelled, and he stood to pedal with all his might. He guessed that the state trooper was less than a quarter mile behind him and could catch him within seconds.

Daniel was near an exit, and he decided to take it. If the trooper saw him heading that way, he probably wouldn't expect him to go across to the entrance and head right back onto the freeway again.

He sensed the spotlight on his back from a distance as he reached the top of the exit ramp. "Stop, Daniel!" Yolanda pleaded, but he flew past the stop sign and down the entrance ramp to the other side, pumping furiously.

The charge up the ramp had nearly taken all his strength and breath, but now Daniel was picking up speed going down onto the freeway. He squinted at his speedometer as they passed under a light. Twenty-five miles an hour, and it probably would have been faster without Yolanda on the crossbar.

In his rearview mirror, he saw the squad car

turn right and slow down, looking for him up on the crossroad. "Keep watching him, Yo-Yo," he said. "If he comes back this way, we'll have to ditch the bike!"

"Then what?" she asked.

"Then we hide in the bushes till he gives up."

"And then?"

"Then we'll walk."

"All the way to the train station?"

"Yup. All the way."

"How far is that?"

"I don't know. Couple of miles, at least."

"Daniel, let's go back."

With that he carefully slowed down and dragged his feet on the shoulder of the road. "Yolanda, if you want to go back, you go now by yourself. I'm going to Grandpa's with or without you. If you're coming with me, you've got to stop begging to go home."

"I can't go back by myself! I'm not sure I know the way."

"Yes, you can. That policeman will find you and take you back."

"Then they'll make me tell where you're going."

"You can't tell them."

"Then I'd better stay with you, Daniel."

"OK, but no more talk about going back," he said.

She nodded miserably. "Daniel," she cried, pointing at the entrance ramp several hundred yards behind them. "Look!"

2

The
Injury

The state police car sat at the top of the entrance ramp looking down onto the freeway, his spotlight slowly covering the area. Daniel knew he and Yolanda were far enough away not to be seen, but if the car started down the ramp, they'd be caught for sure.

He started out again and slowly picked up speed. He hoped to reach the bridge that crossed the highway before the trooper started heading their way.

If they weren't seen, Daniel could ditch the bike behind the huge concrete posts that supported the bridge. Then he and Yo-Yo could hide there until the coast was clear.

He was pumping as hard and fast as he could by the time they reached the safety of the bridge. He stopped and stared back at the entrance ramp, about a half mile away. The police car had slowly rolled across to the other side, still surveying the area.

But he had found nothing and was turning around to come down onto the highway again. Daniel snatched their bags off the handlebars. He told Yolanda to take them up behind the big pillars and wait. "I'll be right there," he said.

He ran with his bike to the edge of the road and down into a soggy ditch where he lay it on its side. Then he scrambled back up and over to the bridge where he joined Yolanda. He couldn't see her face in the blackness, but he knew she was scared.

He put his arm around her. She was shivering. In about a minute, the police car drove by slowly. He had stopped using his spotlight, so Daniel hoped he figured he'd lost them on the overpass.

"I can't risk taking the bike again," he told Yolanda. "We'll have to walk. I've got to move it, though for they'll find it easily if Mom and Dad report us missing and the state trooper remembers seeing us."

"Where are you going to put it, Daniel?"

"Back there. In those bushes."

"Daniel."

"What?"

"My seat is wet and cold."

"Wet? How did you get wet?"

"Aren't you wet, Daniel?"

He felt his seat. Sure enough, the damp earth behind the bridge pillars had ground its way into their jeans. "No time to change now," he said. "Let's get going."

After Daniel had hidden his bike deep in the underbrush, about fifty feet off the highway, they returned to the shoulder and began the slow journey.

He guessed they were about two miles from the train station where they could catch a train into the city. There they would get another train to his grandfather's home, almost two hundred and fifty miles away.

"How long will it take us to get there?" Yolanda asked.

"About four hours," Daniel said, thinking she meant the long ride to Grandpa's.

"Four hours! I thought you said it was only two miles!"

"Oh, you mean into the city? About an hour."

Daniel saw car lights far in the distance. "C'mon," he shouted, and they scampered down the side of the ditch out of sight.

"We've got to be faster than that," Daniel said

as they climbed out again. "By the time we see the cars, they can almost see us."

"But that wasn't a police car."

"We can't trust anyone, Yo-Yo. Nobody expects to see kids out on this highway at this time of the night. In fact, nobody's supposed to be out here except cars and motorcycles."

"What if we get caught?" she asked.

"Don't even say that," Daniel said.

Forty minutes later, and a half dozen more times in the ditch, Daniel and Yolanda were in view of their exit. Suddenly, from behind them, came a whole line of cars and trucks.

They ran down into the ditch again, and Daniel decided that the morning traffic flow was just starting to pick up.

They waited in the ditch for several minutes, but there didn't seem to be any break in the line of cars and trucks. Daniel noticed that the ditch ended near the exit ramp, so they would need a long stretch with no cars to make it up to the road into the city.

It didn't take him long to realize that there would be no more breaks in the traffic, and there'd certainly be no way they could make it up the exit ramp without being seen.

Daniel just hoped his parents hadn't already

noticed he and Yolanda were missing. If people were looking for an eleven-year-old blond boy and a little Mexican girl, they wouldn't be hard to find.

"We're going to have to go through that field back there," he told Yolanda.

"You're kidding," she said, turning to look at the recently harvested grapevines that stood in scary lines in the darkness. "Won't it be muddy?"

"Probably," he said, knowing he would never talk her into it if he didn't just lead the way. He popped up and ran back to the cover of the fence separating the field from the ditch. Yolanda was soon close behind, her skinny little legs churning.

Daniel pulled up short at the base of the fence, gingerly touching the barbs on the wire to see how sharp they were. He slid his fingers between the points and stretched the middle two wires apart, motioning Yo-Yo to step through.

"Careful," he said, as her jacket sleeve caught and tore. "Let me have your bag."

She left the bag with him and made it through. But she wasn't strong enough to hold the wires for Daniel so he could climb through. "I can hold the top one if you can hold the next one," she suggested.

"Never mind," he said, deciding that wouldn't

work. He tossed their bags over and edged down to one of the fence posts.

As Yolanda matched him step for step from the other side, she said the one word that he didn't want to hear. "Muddy."

Daniel put both hands on the top of the post, which was just about his height. He bent low with his right knee and swung his left foot up onto the top wire, between the barbs. Then he let his foot slide across the wire until it was lodged next to one of the sharp points. It wouldn't hurt if the point dug into his rubber sole a little.

With a grunt and a rush, he pushed off with his right foot from the ground first. Then, with his left off the wire, he pushed up and away from the post with both hands. As he flew through the air, he twisted to clear the wire and land, he hoped, on his side or his back.

But in midair his wet shoe slipped off the barb on the top wire. Though his body had already cleared the wire, and he had begun tumbling toward the ground on the other side, the inside of his shin dragged across a barb which dug into him through his thick pants.

He knew he had scratched himself, but he didn't know how badly. At first there was no pain, but, just after he felt the trickle of blood run down into his socks, the burning feeling started. "Oh, how I wish I'd brought a flashlight!" he said.

"I brought one," Yolanda said, her voice weak. She was scared.

"Did you really, Yo-Yo?" he said, surprised. "Shine it over here."

She dug out the light and pointed it at his leg. "Keep it low," he said. "We don't want anyone to see us."

Daniel slowly lifted the leg of his pants, and Yolanda whimpered when she saw that his sock was already red with blood. "Does it hurt bad?" she asked.

Daniel shook his head, but his mouth was shut tight. "Not at all," he said, pulling his jeans up to show the cut. Yolanda couldn't stand it, but Daniel insisted that she hold the light right on it.

"I have to see if it's something I can fix," he said, already wishing he hadn't gotten himself into this mess. But he was not about to give up unless he couldn't walk.

In the bright beam from the flashlight, Daniel pulled a sock from his bag and quickly wiped the blood off his leg. That gave him a better look at the long tear in his leg. He wondered how deep it would have been if it hadn't been for his jeans. They had kept it from going any deeper.

He knew the fence was old and rusty. He knew he should get some kind of a shot to protect himself from infection, but then he would be caught for sure. He prayed silently that his leg wouldn't get infected, and he tied the sock tightly around his shin. It was not so tight that his foot would go to sleep, but tight enough to stop the bleeding.

Somehow, praying while he was doing something that he knew was wrong, something that would scare his parents, something that was going to get him in big trouble, just made Daniel feel worse.

As he got to his feet and realized he could walk, he tried to show Yolanda how brave he was. He picked up both bags and lead her through the muddy rows of grapevines toward the road that would take them to the train station.

By the time they reached the far edge of the field and could see a barn and small farmhouse, they were deep in mud. Also, Daniel was limping badly. He knew if he could just get on solid, dry ground he'd be able to make it.

But as they moved through the backyard of the farmhouse, a loud, gruff voice spoke out in the stillness. It was a voice that would frighten anyone—even an adult.

"I got me a shotgun trained on you! Now who goes there?"

"We're just kids," Yolanda whined before Daniel could stop her.

"Yeah," Daniel said, thinking quickly, "we're trying to find the train station, Sir."

3

Lying

Daniel and Yolanda were frozen where they stood, just a few feet from the end of the grapevines and not far from a gnarled old tree in the yard.

The voice shined a bright, white light in their faces, making them hide their eyes with their hands. A light came on in the house, and an old woman's face peered out from a window.

"Why, you *are* just a coupla kids!" the man said, edging closer. When he turned off his huge flashlight and reached in to turn on the porch light, they could see how old and bent he was.

He wore a yellow raincoat with a hood over long underwear and black rubber boots. As he sloshed slowly through the yard toward them Daniel noticed that he didn't have a shotgun.

Maybe he had put it inside when he'd turned on the light.

"Do whatever I do," Daniel whispered to Yolanda.

"What's that you say?" the old man said. "You two liked to scared me to death comin' through here. I was just checkin' to see if my paper was here, but it's too early."

Daniel took off like a shot, running as fast as his injured leg would carry him. He ran past the old man, around to the front of the house, and into the road, his bags flapping against his side as he ran.

"Where ya goin'?" the old man yelled. "I ain't gonna hurt ya! I ain't got no gun!"

Daniel whirled around when he didn't hear Yolanda following him. He didn't want to call out her name, in case the old man reported seeing them.

"C'mere little girl," the man said. Then Yolanda ran off faster than Daniel, passing him on the road. He struggled to keep up, limping worse than ever now.

"Dumb, fool kids," they heard the old man mutter before he slammed the door.

Yolanda couldn't help but chuckle. But when she saw her brother struggling to just walk, she took the bags from him. "We didn't tell him the truth, Daniel. That makes me feel very bad."

"Me, too," he admitted. "But I didn't want him to keep us from getting to Grandpa's."

"Am I going to like your grandpa, Daniel?"

"Sure you are. He's your grandpa now, too. I just wish you could have known Grandma Bradford before she died."

"Will your grandpa fix your leg?"

"Sure. At least he'll get me to a doctor without me getting in trouble."

"We're already in trouble, Daniel."

"I know."

His leg was throbbing from the ankle to the knee, but he knew his way to the train station from where they were. "Just up that hill and around the bend, then we can cut through a big park. I want to get there before dawn, because that's when all the business people take the trains into the city."

They scraped the mud from their feet as they hurried along. Yolanda's feet were beginning to hurt. She hadn't walked so far so fast for a long time. But now that Daniel sensed he was close to the train station, he seemed to move even faster.

He was hurt, but his longer legs still carried him ahead of her. She had to run a little to keep up. Then it began to rain.

"Oh, no, Daniel, it's getting so cold!" she said.

"C'mon, put this over your head," he said, pulling another sweatshirt from his bag. He pulled the hood up on the one he was wearing and kept trudging along, hoping and praying that the drizzle wouldn't turn into a big downpour.

All the while he kept thinking that if people would only trust him, would only believe him when he told them the truth, he wouldn't be in this mess. Maybe it wasn't the right thing to do, but he didn't have a choice, did he?

A guy couldn't stay in a place where he wasn't trusted, could he? Maybe he shouldn't have dragged Yolanda into it, but she was the only one who believed him. He needed someone with him who was on his side. If he'd headed for Grandpa's without her, it would have been pretty lonely.

And what if there had been no one to hold the flashlight so he could see if he was fixing up his leg correctly? In fact, if it hadn't been for her, he wouldn't have even had a flashlight. He wondered if God could be watching out for him, even when he was doing something like this.

Maybe to Yolanda the rain was cold, but to Daniel, who had grown warm with the struggle of walking on his bad leg, it felt good. After a while, when they went up a small hill and could see the big park from the top, he pulled his hood back and let the rain fall on his head and neck.

Yolanda huddled next to him, shivering. "You okay, Yo-Yo?" he asked. She nodded, but he wasn't so sure. "Let's keep moving. It'll be warm in the station."

It was just after five o'clock in the morning when they walked into the waiting area. A janitor looked them over carefully, but he said nothing when Daniel pretended to know just what he was doing.

He'd been here before. He, his mother, Jim, and Maryann had taken the train into the city many times for special things. Holidays. Shopping. To meet Dad.

and sister made Daniel homesick already. But since he had come this far, dodged the police, hidden his bike, cut himself, sloshed through a muddy field, outrun an old farmer, and made it to the station in the rain, he wouldn't be turning back now.

Daniel walked up to the schedule board and looked for the outbound trains to the city. There was one in a little over ten minutes. He thought up a story for the man at the ticket counter. He felt the same sick feeling in the pit of his stomach that he had felt when he talked to the farmer. He would tell the ticket seller that his mother was in the restroom, and that he would be buying all three tickets, one adult and two children.

That would satisfy the man for sure, and it would keep him from asking what Daniel and his little sister were doing there all alone. As long as the janitor didn't overhear, and tell the ticket man that he had seen them come in alone, they would be all right.

But when they reached the counter, Daniel's plan couldn't work. There was no ticket seller this early in the morning. The sign said that riders on the trains before six-thirty were to buy their tickets on the train.

Now his plan would be a little trickier. How was he supposed to pull it off without an adult with him? What was he supposed to tell the conductor? He thought about it as he and Yolanda went back out into the cold rain and stood on the platform.

Several minutes later, when the engine light came into view around the far turn, Daniel realized that he and his little sister were standing on the wrong side of the platform to board the train.

If the engineer saw no one standing on the right platform, he would stop only briefly and

She didn't make it.

take off right away. Daniel wondered if he should wave at the conductor or yell or what? He didn't know.

He knew it was not wise to run across two other sets of tracks to get to the right side, but it was the only way he knew of being sure to get on the train. The next one wasn't for another hour, and it would be loaded with business people.

But then they could be caught, on their way home, or punished. And he wouldn't have had a chance to tell Grandpa his story and convince him that he had been telling the truth all along. He needed Grandpa, somebody, anybody, to be on his side.

He grabbed Yolanda's hand and ran to the end of the platform. "We've got to get to the other side!" he yelled as the train whistle blew, and the tracks and the platform steps vibrated from the rumbling of the engine.

"We'll never make it, Daniel!" Yolanda said, tripping as he dragged her along.

As they darted across the first set of tracks, her hand slipped from his grip. Daniel kept going and leaped onto the ties in the middle of the third set of tracks, then up onto the platform on the other side, tossing his bag ahead of him.

He turned to look for Yolanda, but she had fallen onto the number two track. She was just getting up as the train chugged in. "Stay there, Yo-Yo!" Daniel screamed. "Don't try to make it!"

It looked to him as if she stepped into the path of the train as it whizzed by him. He ran toward the engine, dreading what he might see.

The conductor saw him running, and Daniel hoped he would keep the train from starting again until he knew what had happened to Yolanda. He knew he didn't want to see the front of the train if it had hit her.

He jumped off the side of the platform and dropped to his knees to peer underneath. He hoped he would see her still crouched on track two, waiting for the train to pass.

But she wasn't there!

4

The
Train
Ride

Frantically, Daniel leaped to his feet and searched the windows. He was looking for the puzzled face of the conductor who had been staring at him before he jumped off the platform.

Daniel didn't see him at first, so he ran back and forth, dropping to all fours here and there to see if he could see Yolanda on the other side of the train.

He finally realized he had to get around to the other side, no matter what he might find. So he ran on the gravel in the narrow passageway between the train and the platform.

As he passed the first passenger car behind the engine, the conductor leaned out the wide doors. "What're you doin' there, boy?" he demanded. "You gotta git up on the platform!"

"My sister!" Daniel yelled, out of breath and still running, limping near to the front of the engine. "My sister!"

When he heard him, the conductor hopped back into the car and stuck a metal key into a special box that locked the brakes. This signaled the engineer to wait.

Daniel was just about to stagger around the front, hoping the train wouldn't start moving, when Yolanda came running around from the other side. She ran right into him. They almost knocked each other down.

He was so glad to see her that he hardly knew what to say. "I fell," she said. "I'm sure glad you told me to wait, because I almost ran in front of the train!"

He grabbed her hand, pulled her up onto the platform, and led her down to the entrance of the first passenger car. The conductor saw them and pulled the key from the box. Then he signaled the engineer that all was clear.

"Wait." Daniel yelled, scooping up his bag. "Let us on."

The conductor tried to wave them off, but Daniel hung onto Yolanda and leaped onto the steps, just before the train began to slowly pull out. They held tightly to the handrails outside the closed door, and the conductor had to open it so they wouldn't fall onto the tracks below.

"I'm not s'posed to let kids on here!" he said as they moved past and found a seat. "Where do you think you're going?"

"It's only twenty-one minutes into the city," Daniel said, thinking fast and remembering the schedule board. "We'll be getting off there."

The conductor looked at them suspiciously as they sat down. "That'll be three sixty each, Sonny," he said.

"It will not," Daniel said, surprising even himself. "We're both under twelve, so it's half price."

"That's only during the day and when you're with a full-paying adult or guardian," the conductor said. Daniel looked worried and pretended to cry.

"What's your problem, Kid? Don't you have enough money?" the conductor asked.

"I don't think we should have to pay full fare for such a short trip," Daniel said.

"Oh, yeah? Why not?"

"Because my sister has no money, Sir," he said.

"No money! Is someone going to meet you kids when you get to the city? Does anyone know you're coming?" the conductor asked.

Daniel panicked. He hadn't expected all these

questions. Lying wasn't easy. And keeping track of all his made-up stories wasn't either.

"OK," the conductor said, "Gimme, four bucks and we'll call it even. But there better be somebody waitin' for you in the city, or you'll be answerin' to me."

As the conductor strolled back through the other cars, Daniel wondered if there really were other people riding into the city at this time of the night. Or, he should say, at this time of the morning.

"We've got to get off before he sees that there's no one meeting us," Daniel said. Yolanda shook her head slowly. "What's the matter with you?" Daniel asked.

"Nothing," she said, turning away.

"C'mon," Daniel said, "What is it?"

"You're not telling the truth, Daniel!" she said, turning back and staring at him. "I've lost count of the number of times you've lied."

Daniel pressed his lips together tightly and stared out the window into the blackness. He felt terrible. He wanted to tell her that there was a reason for it all. For if he told the true story, they would be caught and returned home, where no one believed him or trusted him except her.

Only Daniel knew that Yolanda was not trusting him anymore either, because there was never a really good reason to lie. If he was able to lie about so many things on this strange night, when they had hardly begun their trip to Grandpa's, maybe she was wondering if he had lied at home in the first place.

But that was just it. He hadn't. He was innocent. How could he ever prove it now? He didn't even have time to think about it. His leg ached, he was dead tired, he was scared, and he had to think of how to get away from the conductor. And now he felt so guilty for lying, especially in front of his little sister.

Yolanda looked up to Daniel. She always had. In fact, she loved going to church and Sunday school, and she had been asking him what Jesus meant when he said, "Let the little children come to me. Do not prevent them."

He wanted to tell her all about it. He prayed for her and asked his dad to say things right so Yolanda would love Jesus like he did. But now this. He was not acting like someone who really loved Jesus. He was being a terrible example.

When this whole mess was cleared up, and he hoped Grandpa could somehow help straighten it all out, he was going to have to go back to the farmer and to the conductor and tell them the truth. But before he did that, he would have to

They were almost there.

pray and ask God for His forgiveness first.

He hoped Grandpa would believe him, but there was little time to think about that now. He had to find a way to get himself and Yolanda off the train without facing the conductor.

Yolanda was still staring at him with those huge dark eyes of hers, waiting for him to say something about all his lying.

"I'm sorry," he said. "When we get to Grandpa's I'll straighten it all out."

Her eyes filled with tears, but she didn't let them fall. "I never want to get used to you lying," she said. "Never."

And that only made Daniel feel worse.

As the train began to slow down at the big depot in town, Daniel studied the chart on the wall near the ceiling. Its red and blue lines showed where they were to go to switch from the commuter train to the big passenger train that would take them on the four-hour journey to Grandpa Bradford's.

Daniel leaned against the window and shielded his eyes with his hand, so he could see outside. As the train entered the depot, he backed away from the side window and peered through the window at the end of their car, trying to see where the conductor was.

Sure enough, he was coming through the cars

toward Daniel and Yolanda. He was about four cars away, moving quickly, pausing only for the automatic doors to open.

"Hang on and brace yourself. Then follow me," Daniel said, hoisting his bag over his left shoulder and moving toward the door.

"What are you going to do, Daniel?" Yolanda asked in a frightened voice.

"Just do what I say," he said, as he climbed up on a seat and grabbed the metal key.

"Daniel, no!" Yolanda cried.

He looked out the window once more and saw that they were about a hundred yards from the end of the track. The conductor was now at the far end of the next car, hurrying toward them.

Daniel reached up and plunged the key into the special box that locked the brakes on the train. It caused a horrible screeching sound as the whole train ground slowly to a stop. Yolanda hung on as he told her, but her bag flew from her hands and slid down the aisle. She was able to grab hold of it just in time.

Daniel lost his grip and fell heavily from his perch on the seat. He yelped as all his weight was put on his injured leg. He fell into the small stairwell. The doors opened automatically as the conductor worked his way through from the next car.

Daniel jumped from the train to a cement platform just inside the depot. He began to run, as well as he could with his throbbing leg, toward the big lobby. Yolanda was right behind him, dragging her bag.

The conductor jumped off and started chasing the children, but the engineer's whistle blast made him think better of it. He returned to the train just as it started again.

Daniel didn't quit running until he was within sight of the track where they would board the next train. Then he took time to look at the schedule board. A train to Grandpa's town was leaving in less than twenty minutes.

If he could keep them from being caught until then, Daniel could get on the train, tell his story, and maybe get some sleep. He wanted to find a bathroom and get a closer look at his leg, too.

Most of all, he needed time to think, to remind himself of all the trouble he'd been in at home. He wondered if the memory of it would make him feel better about all the bad things he had done wrong in order to get to see Grandpa.

At least he hoped so.

5

More
Lies

In the waiting area, Daniel found chairs behind large, round pillars. He sat where he was able to see anyone coming towards them before being seen.

"Daniel," Yolanda said wearily, "does that sign mean we have to buy our tickets before we get on the train?"

A sign near the entrance to the train platform read: Do Not Board Without Ticket.

Daniel nodded, a look of frustration on his face. He didn't think he could walk anymore until he had some rest. He spotted the ticket counter from where he sat.

"Yo-Yo," he said, "here's some money. Go over there and get in line. Then ask for two children's tickets. It should be about fifty dollars."

"What can I do for you?"

He watched anxiously as Yolanda waited in line. She looked scared. Daniel kept looking all around to make sure no one was coming to ask him what they were doing there without an adult.

Then it was Yolanda's turn. The woman at the counter leaned way over and looked at her. It was obvious to Daniel that she was asking a lot of questions. Yolanda keep turning around and looking at Daniel, but each time he looked away.

Finally, she came running back to him, crying. "I'm sorry, Daniel," she said, giving him the money. "I can't do it. She asked where my mother or dad were, and I didn't know what to say."

"You didn't tell her, did you?" he demanded.

"No! I didn't know what to say, so I spoke in Spanish."

"You what?" Daniel said. He was amazed and impressed.

"First, I asked for the tickets with a Spanish accent. Then when she asked all those questions, I spoke Spanish. She said she was going to get someone who could understand me, so I came back here."

"That was great, Yo-Yo!" he said, looking at the clock. He realized that they didn't have much time. "Stay right here and don't let anyone take our stuff."

50

He limped over to the ticket counter, wondering about what he would say. It scared him to think how easily he seemed to come up with his wild stories. He knew not telling the truth had a way of catching up with people, for he was already in trouble for lies that someone else had told on him.

"I'm sorry my friend didn't understand you," he told the woman.

"I didn't understand *her* either, Honey," she said. "Now what do you kids want?"

"Two tickets for the number five train."

"That's a four-hour ride, young man. We can't let you kids on alone."

"Oh, uh, we won't be alone," Daniel said, thinking quickly. "My mother will be with us. She's coming soon, but she wanted me to get our tickets. She already has hers."

The woman looked doubtful but slowly pulled two tickets from a drawer. "That will be twenty-two each if you're under twelve. You are under twelve, aren't you?"

"Yes, ma'am. I won't be twelve until next year."

The woman held the tickets in her hand, and Daniel slid the forty-four dollars across the counter to her. Still she hesitated. "I'm sorry, Son, but I need to know if that is your mother over there?"

Daniel's heart sank. He slowly turned toward Yolanda. She was sitting with an older woman — definitely not his mother. The woman was dressed in a heavy coat, and she was holding two shopping bags on her lap.

He panicked, wondering what she wanted, and what Yolanda might have said to her. He wanted to run over and rescue Yo-Yo from her, but then how would they get to Grandpa's? He didn't know how to get to the bus station, or even if there was a bus to Grandpa's town. He didn't know if they could ride a bus without a parent, either.

Yolanda and the woman looked over at Daniel. Much to his surprise, they both waved at him. "See her," he said to the woman at the counter as he waved back.

The woman scowled and took his money, shoving the tickets across the counter to him. When he got back to Yolanda, the woman smiled at him. "I was just askin' your friend here if she had a little spare change for a hungry lady," she said.

"You want money?" Daniel said. "I just spent the last of my money for train tickets."

"All your money?" she asked. "Every last cent? Your friend here said that if I waved at you, you might give me some money."

Daniel gave Yolanda a dirty look, even though he realized that she had helped him a lot. "I might have a dollar left," he said. Reaching inside his jacket, he felt the wad of bills, just a little less than half of what he started out with.

He carefully peeled one bill from the rest. "You could do me one more favor," he said, "and then I'll give you the dollar."

"Make it two and I'll do anything you say," she said.

"I just want you to walk to the train with us, and don't come back here to the lobby until the train leaves."

She studied his face. "You're not traveling with an adult," she said finally.

"That's none of your business," he said.

"None of my business, you say? It'd be my business if I marched over there and told the ticket seller, now wouldn't it? And it'd be my business if I told the conductor!"

"All right," Daniel said, exasperated. "So it's your business. We're traveling alone. So what?"

"So I'm going to need three dollars to convince the conductor that I'm with you, and to get away without getting on the train. And don't tell me you haven't got three dollars, because you're not goin' far without money."

"Okay, then, come on," Daniel said.

Yolanda slowly lugged her bag from the seat. Daniel rose slowly on his injured leg. The bag woman struggled to her feet and shuffled along to the platform with them. "Here's the plan," she said.

"The plan?" Daniel repeated.

"Just listen," she said. "You two get on the very first car and start walking through the cars to the other end of the train. Tell anyone who asks that you're meeting your mom in the next car. I'll keep walking along the platform, and, if the conductor asks me, I'll tell him I'm getting on the next car. As soon as he gets busy with everyone else, I'll just head back to the station."

"But you won't go into the lobby until the train leaves, will you? The woman at the ticket counter thinks you're going with us. I'll bet she could have the train stopped if she saw you weren't on it."

"Don't worry about me," she said. "Just give me my three bucks and follow the plan."

It worked perfectly. By the time the train pulled out, Daniel and Yolanda had reached the seventh car and had been asked only once where their mother or father was.

Daniel chose an almost empty car, told the ticket taker their mother had given them per mission to sit in this car, and tossed their bags on the racks above their heads.

The seats, actually wide enough for three adults, gave them plenty of room to stretch out. Yolanda sat behind Daniel, putting her hands on top of the back of his seat and resting her chin on her hands.

"I'm tired," she said. "And hungry."

"We'll get something soon," he said.

"How's your leg, Daniel?"

"Fine," he said. It was the biggest lie he had told since they'd left home.

The truth was, the pain was deep and burning. He was afraid that if he didn't get to a doctor soon, he might really be in trouble. Daniel couldn't believe how exhausted he felt.

"I'm going to sleep for a while if I can," he told Yolanda. "You going to be all right?"

She nodded, almost crying. "I don't like this much," she said.

"But you know why I'm doing it, right?" he asked.

"I guess so."

"You guess so? You don't think I'm doing what I have to do?"

She shrugged.

"C'mon, Yo-Yo," he said, sitting up. "I have to know you're still with me. "

She fought to keep from crying. Staring at him with those big dark eyes, she slowly lowered herself out of his sight and lay down on the seat.

Daniel felt terrible. He lay down, too, but sleep was impossible. With the gentle rocking of the train, and the steady noise of the wheels clacking along the track, the only other sound Daniel heard was Yolanda's quiet weeping in the seat behind him.

As he covered his eyes to keep out the harsh morning sun, all he could think of was how he had gotten into this mess in the first place.

6

The Science Project

Daniel had had much to be proud of the month before when school started.

He was going into the sixth grade, the last grade before entering junior high. And he would be one of the starters on the basketball team in a few months.

His older sister Maryann was a sophomore at the high school, and she had just made the varsity cheerleading team.

His older brother Jim was a senior and was a starter on the varsity basketball team for the third straight year. He was the best player the school had ever had, and everyone knew that he would be all-league, all-area, all-district, all-state, and maybe even high school all-American.

Daniel also had a newly adopted sister going into the fourth grade, and she was beautiful.

Except for a few unkind remarks by some jealous kids about her brown skin, and the fact that she had been adopted by a white family, Yo-Yo quickly became a favorite of most everyone. Daniel was proud of her.

In fact, Daniel had just about everything he wanted. He was popular, he thought. He was one of the brighter students in his class. His father was a test pilot who often worked at the space center in Florida, and who knew several astronauts.

Daniel was happy. He enjoyed his life and his school, his church and Sunday school, and his home and family. He had always wanted a brother or sister more his own age, because Jim and Maryann were older. Now he had one.

What could be better? He had gone through some tough times when he was in the second grade because he had told a lie. He had told his mother something belonged to him when it didn't. It really had belonged to his older brother, but Daniel had insisted it belonged to him.

"I'll have to punish you if I find out you are lying," his mother had told him. "And I'll have to tell your father when he gets home."

"Okay, fine," Daniel had said. "Because I'm telling the truth."

But his conscience had begun to work on him,

and, within less than an hour, he felt terrible. He had gone to his mother and told her the truth. "You *can* punish me," he said, "and you *can* tell Dad."

By then he *wanted* the punishment, so he could feel clean again. Also he had prayed for forgiveness from God. He had been ashamed, and he had been worried whether or not God and his parents would still love him as much as ever. But they had assured him they did, and he had been sure he was cured of lying. For good.

But now, less than four years later, his world had come crashing down around him. He had been accused of dishonesty again. Cheating. Only this time it wasn't true. He was innocent. Totally innocent. And no one believed him. No one but Yo-Yo.

It had been on a Monday morning, about a month into the new school year, when Daniel presented his science project. He had been working on it since the first week of school, carefully building it in the basement at home.

The whole family had been impressed with the project from the beginning. It was a miniature solar-powered city — built to scale.

He could interview his father or any other expert he wanted. And he could read about and research the project anywhere, but the final product had to be all his own. No copying at all.

The project became so big that everyone in the family enjoyed watching it grow. Week after week, Daniel added more and more. Carefully he cut the wood and metal and plastic and handled all the electrical wiring himself.

Daniel was more and more excited as the big day approached. His dad would drive him to school and help him carry the model community into the class. Then his dad would go to the airport for one of his trips to Florida.

Daniel was ready. The city looked real, and, best of all, when plugged in it really worked. Any kind of light, sunlight or even the lights in his classroom, would activate the solar batteries he had constructed.

Then everything would begin to work. Little traffic lights, automatic doors, fans, streetlights, train crossing signals, everything. Daniel had prepared a speech to explain it all — along with a long, written report.

He had never been the smartest kid in his class, though he had always done well. Science was his favorite subject. The year before his project had been judged second best in the class and third best in the school.

This time he couldn't imagine anyone doing anything better. He wasn't proud in a show-off way, and he was careful not to brag about it, but he just knew he had *the best* project this year.

Daniel enjoyed getting to school early with his dad. His teacher let them in to set up. Mrs. Quarry had the janitor bring in a long table and place it at the front of the class. "Your presentation will be after lunch," she told Daniel, "so we'll keep it covered until then."

Daniel and his dad worked quickly to set everything up. Then they carefully draped an old blanket over the whole thing. "You remember what you told me about trying to memorize my report, so I could explain it without reading, Dad?"

Mr. Bradford nodded.

"I did that."

"Really? You're ready to do it without having to look at your notes?"

"Yup."

"I'm proud of you, Daniel. I wish I could be here to hear you give it."

"I'm glad you won't be, Dad. I'd be too nervous! I probably will be too nervous even without you here."

"Maybe Mom could come, Dan."

"No! She already promised she wouldn't. Really. I just want to get it over with."

"You sound like you're not excited about it,

It's a secret.

Dan. What seems to be the problem?"

"I am, Dad. You know that. It's just that this isn't like a ball game or a play or something. It's not the kind of thing that parents come to watch. You know what I mean? You know Scotty Majors?"

His dad nodded. "The boy who won last year and finished second in the whole school?"

"Yeah. His parents didn't come when he did his last week. None of the parents have been here."

"Okay, then. I just wanted you to know that we'd be here if we could — and if you wanted us."

"I know, Dad, and thanks."

Daniel walked his dad out to the car as Mrs. Quarry headed for the teachers' lounge. Other kids started showing up at their lockers. "Hi Amy!" Daniel said shyly. "Hi Scotty, hey Bill, hi Tim."

"You ready for your big speech today, Dan?" Tim asked.

"I guess."

"That your dad?"

"Yeah. Dad, this is Tim, and you know Scotty and Bill and Amy."

"I sure do. Hi kids. Nice to meet you, Tim."

More kids were coming — all curious about Daniel's famous dad. His picture had been in the papers several times. There had been talk also in the past years about him becoming an astronaut and going on a space mission.

"You gonna come and speak to our class again sometime, Mr. Bradford?" Scott Majors called after them as they neared the door.

"Oh, you never know," Mr. Bradford said. "If your teacher invites me, I just might."

Daniel was embarrassed when his dad put his arm around him in the parking lot. "Dad, not here in front of all the kids!" he said.

"Oh, sorry, Dan," he said. "I forgot you're getting a little too big for that in public, aren't you?"

Daniel nodded.

"Listen, Dan, I just want you to know how proud Mom and I are of all the work you did on this project. So, no matter how it turns out, you should be happy about it."

"What do you mean, Dad? You know how it turned out."

"I know, but I mean your presentation today and everything. That's all part of the grade, isn't it?"

"Yeah, but I'd have to do pretty bad on my speech to get a bad grade on this project, don't you think?"

"I suppose. I just don't want you to be nervous.

Don't worry about if it's first place or not."

"I know I shouldn't, but I do. I mean, I didn't build it just to win, Dad. But when it came out so nice, well, I have to think I have a good chance, and I *would* be disappointed if it wasn't the best. Scotty already did his, and it was good, but it was nothing like mine. Amy's will probably be good, too, but she has never won."

"Well, Dan, good luck today. I know you'll do well, and I'm impressed that you're going to do it without notes."

"Thanks, Dad. Have a good trip. When are you coming home?"

"Friday night in time for dinner. See you then."

Little did Daniel know that his Dad would be back the very next evening. And because of bad, bad news.

7

Daniel's Presentation

Daniel had grown more and more nervous throughout the morning. When he returned to his classroom, and saw several kids milling around his table — as if trying to work up enough courage to peek beneath the blanket —he hardly knew what to say.

He wasn't brave enough to tell them off, so he just walked up and stood next to the table, as if daring them to try anything. Scotty Majors, who was already sitting at his desk, said, "Oh, what's the matter, Bradford? Afraid somebody's gonna hurt your toy city?"

Daniel didn't answer. He never answered Scotty when he was being sarcastic. He had learned that from his mother. She always said that if you didn't answer someone who was being mean, they would remember longer what they said and how terrible it sounded.

But Daniel did wonder how Scotty had guessed he had a town under the blanket. He stared at it, wondering if it was obvious to everybody. He had told no one.

During recess that morning, Daniel's team had beaten Scotty's team, because Scotty and Amy left after a few minutes, saying they had something to do.

Daniel worried about them, because he didn't want them to miss his presentation. Even though he was nervous about it, he had to admit he wanted everyone to see and hear it.

Just before lunch he prayed silently, asking God to help him remember everything and to be clear in his presentation. He put the written report in his desk and left it there. He would give it to Mrs. Quarry at the end of the day.

After lunch he didn't get in the usual softball game, because he wanted to run through his speech again in his mind. Scotty wasn't playing either, so it didn't even matter to Daniel who won. He got as much enjoyment out of beating Scotty's team as anything.

Daniel had worked himself up into a state of nervousness by the time one o'clock rolled around. When Mrs. Quarry called on him, he almost shouted, "Yes, ma'am!" and he tripped on his way up to the front.

Several kids giggled, but he composed himself and began to take the blanket off his project. Mrs. Quarry saw that he needed help, but before she could get to him, Scotty Majors jumped up and ran to the front. He grabbed the other end of the blanket and yanked it off.

"Thank you, Scott," Mrs. Quarry said, "but do be careful."

Nothing seemed to suffer from Scotty's roughness, but Daniel was horrified to see that one of his miniature solar plates was bent and broken away from its base. It must have happened when he and his dad carried it in, because it was on the end where he had lifted the blanket, and he knew he hadn't dragged anything across it.

Quickly he bent it back into position and made sure the metal frame was touching the metal base. That way the electricity would flow correctly. "Whenever you're ready, Daniel," his teacher said.

"Uh-huh," he said, noticing another problem. A loose wire from his main building was sticking out. It was supposed to run through the transformer. It could have been pulled away when the blanket was removed, but, again, it was near Daniel's end and he would have noticed.

Everything had been preassembled at home and was working perfectly. How could those two things have come loose? What was going on? He hurriedly looked over the rest of the project to make sure there wasn't any other damage that would cause it not to work properly.

A plastic housing unit was crushed, but as far as he could tell, that wouldn't hurt anything. "Daniel, please begin," Mrs. Quarry said, a little more firmly this time.

"Yes," he said. "Uh, just let me get my paper." He had been so shaken by the damage to his project that he had forgotten how his speech was supposed to begin. He hadn't promised anyone he would recite it rather than read it.

But he couldn't find it in his desk! He knew it was there! He had put it there himself! Mrs. Quarry stood as he noisily searched through all his papers. He realized he was going to have to go without it and find it later.

"Daniel, surely you finished your paper!"

"Yes ma'am, but I wanted to try to give my presentation without it."

"Oh, my, that would be wonderful. Please proceed."

On his way back to the front of the class, Daniel prayed earnestly, "Lord, please help me keep calm and not worry about my project or my paper. Just help me remember. If someone's trying to play a joke on me, help me show them I can handle it anyway."

As he got to the front of the classroom, he noticed his teacher's admiring glance. Probably a student had never given a science project speech before without reading it. Some of the students looked impressed already, too, even though Scotty and a few of the others sat there looking bored. Daniel decided to put them out of his mind and do the best he could.

Once he was started, he felt as if God had reminded him just where to begin. It went smoothly. His heartbeat slowed a little, he quit shaking, and his voice grew stronger. He was more confident.

He began by saying, "My idea was to build a solar-powered community to prove that . . ." Ten minutes later he was finishing up. He had not missed a point, and he was ready to turn on the power.

"I'll pull the blinds and use only the overhead lights as a source of fuel," he said. When the blinds were pulled, he turned off the room lights and let the students get used to the semidarkness.

"You can clearly see the model community," he said. Several students in the back giggled, but they stood so they could see better. "Now I'll turn on the current, for, as you'll see, nothing will work until the power is generated. And that will come from the lights."

He turned on the power. Then he went over to the light switch and turned on the lights. The students squinted as the room brightened. Immediately everything in the model community began shining, moving, buzzing, and turning. The students clapped.

Daniel smiled and moved back to the blinds. "The more light, the more power," he announced, and he opened the blinds. His model was alive with motion.

Daniel turned off the current and returned to his seat. "Excellent," Mrs. Quarry said. "Just excellent. I'm sure everyone agrees we have at least one entry in the science contest already."

But not everyone looked as thrilled as she did.

The teacher talked on and on about how nice Daniel's model looked, and about how much work must have gone into it. She also said how impressive it was that he had memorized his speech.

Daniel was smiling so big that it almost hurt his mouth. In the excitement, he almost forgot that he had to find his paper. Just before afternoon break was over, he hurried back to his desk to search for it. He had to find it.

He didn't have to search! He could hardly believe it. It was right between his two colored folders, where he had looked not an hour before. He decided he must have just been too nervous and in too much of a hurry.

At the end of the day, he delivered his paper to Mrs. Quarry. She embarrassed him by telling him once again how proud she was of him. "If you put that much effort into every subject, Daniel, you'd be a straight A student."

He nodded shyly. While he waited for the school bus, several students from his class congratulated him and asked how long his project would stay at school. "I guess until after the all-school judging," he said. "And Mrs. Quarry wants other classes to come and see it."

That night Jim and Maryann and Daniel's mom were eager to hear all about it. "I can hardly believe you did that all by yourself," Yolanda said, beaming.

"I know what you mean, Yo-Yo," Jim said. "I've been watching that thing get bigger and bigger and wondering where Daniel got all those ideas. You never even let Dad help you, did you, Dan?"

"Not even me!" Yolanda said. And everyone smiled.

"Where *did* you get all your ideas, Daniel?" Maryann asked.

"Oh, just from lots of studying and stuff. You could read any books you wanted, but your project had to be your own. Um, creation, you know. And nobody could help you."

At least, for that night at dinner, they all were thrilled for him. And they believed him!

8

Called to the Office

Daniel had trouble sleeping that night. He couldn't settle down. Finally, he got up and wandered downstairs where his older sister was reading and his older brother was watching a game on television.

"What are you doing up, Dan?" his mother asked.

"I don't know," he said. "Just excited I guess."

"I'm sure you are, but you've got to get some sleep. Yolanda has been asleep for a couple of hours."

"No she hasn't. I was talking to her about a half hour ago."

"Daniel! Let her sleep! She needs her rest. I know you've had a big, exciting day, and we're all happy for you, but I want you to stay up there and be still. You'll fall asleep soon enough."

74

"You know what I wish, Mom?"

"Tell me, and then get to bed."

"I wish my model community were here so I could just play with it. I worked so hard on it, worrying so much about making it right, that I never really got a chance to just enjoy it. You know what I mean?"

"Yes! Now please get up to bed. It's way past your bedtime."

The phone rang. "Oh, Mom! If that's Dad let me talk to him."

She sighed. "If you promise to go straight to bed right afterwards. No waiting until I'm through."

"Okay, sure, I promise!"

Maryann had answered the phone. "It's your boyfriend, Mom," she said with a twinkle in her eye.

"Hi, Honey," Mom said. "Let Daniel tell you about his big day, and then make him get to bed, will you? Thanks."

Daniel and his dad enjoyed several minutes of chatting about how well things had gone. "When I get home Friday night, the whole family will go out to celebrate, huh, Dan? How's that sound? You pick the place."

"All right! Thanks, Dad!"

"Now get to bed."

We'll all go out and celebrate!

"You and Mom sound alike."

"There's a reason for that, Pal. Now get going. I'm happy for you, and proud of you."

Daniel was dead tired when he awoke on Tuesday morning. He hadn't gone to sleep for another hour and a half after he talked to his dad. Now he was moping around, trying to work up enough energy to get through breakfast and catch the bus.

At school some of the kids in his class were still making a fuss over his great presentation the day before. His teacher told him before class that she had already entered an "A" for him in her grade book.

But Daniel noticed a difference in her later in the morning. At recess when he had asked her something, she seemed to almost ignore him, as if she had something else on her mind.

At lunchtime it seemed to him that she was angry with him, or disappointed in him, or something. He couldn't figure it out. It was almost as if she was pretending he wasn't there. It was a big change from the last day and a half.

Finally, just before the end of the lunch period, she came to him. "Daniel," she began very seriously, "I would like to meet you in the

77

principal's office during the afternoon break. Okay?"

"Sure, what's up?"

"We'll discuss it there."

That sounded like trouble, and Daniel worried about it for a little while, but he decided his teacher had a nice surprise for him and didn't want to give it away.

What else could it be? He had been in no trouble. His science project was probably the best the school had ever seen, at least since Scotty Majors' older brother Ken had won the state prize two years in a row. He had also placed in the national competition once. Ken was already in college, but his picture still hung in the trophy case in the hall.

Maybe that was it. The principal had been so thrilled with Mrs. Quarry's story of Daniel's presentation that he was insisting that it be entered in the state competition. Daniel began to get that tingling sensation in the small of his back, the one he always got when something good was about to happen.

By ten minutes to two, Daniel could hardly wait for the meeting. Mrs. Quarry had not seemed any different during the early part of the afternoon. She had even called on him to answer a couple of questions when he raised his hand to let her know he knew the answer.

He even thought about telling a couple of his friends, but he decided against it, just in case. Maybe it wasn't going to be as good as he thought. Maybe it was just that the principal was going to congratulate him.

During the break, Mrs. Quarry nodded to him and left the room. He ran to the bathroom, and then hurried toward the principal's office. He had always been a little afraid of Mr. Estes, who had taught at the school for thirty years before he became principal. Daniel had never been called to the office for anything bad, but he reminded himself to smile at the giant man with the white hair.

As he walked up the steps leading to the office, he glanced out the window. Something familiar caught his eye. It was his mother's station wagon!

So it *was* state competition! They *were* going to enter his project in the big contest! The school contest hadn't even been held yet, but they were so sure he would win that they were ready to announce the good news. And they wanted his mother here.

As he stepped into the office, and was greeted by the receptionist, he was grinning from ear to ear, almost laughing. "Mr. Estes will see you now," the woman said. "And let me give you a little advice. Wipe that smile off your face."

"Oh," he said, almost winking at her. She didn't want him to appear too overconfident. He put on as serious a look as he could and followed her into the inner office.

His mother sat with her head down, a tissue wadded in her hand. His teacher looked at him sadly, her chin resting in her hands. Mr. Estes stood, towering over Daniel. He spoke in a big, deep voice.

"Sit down please, Mr. Bradford," he said. "Thank you, Miss Tracy."

The receptionist left and shut the door. As Daniel sat down, all thoughts of his science project flew from his mind. All he could think of was that something must have happened to someone in his family.

If it had been Yolanda, he would have known. He would have heard the sirens or seen all the activity. News like that traveled fast around a small school.

"Dad?" he said weakly, staring at his mother.

She shook her head without looking up.

"Jim?"

Again she shook her head. Why wouldn't she look at him? She dabbed at her eyes.

"Maryann — ?"

Mr. Estes interrupted. "Young man," he said as he sat down, "the problem is no one else in your family. The problem is you."

"Me?"

"Please don't compound your mistake by pretending not to know what the problem is."

"But I don't," Daniel said, almost in tears.

"And don't insult me by crying," Mr. Estes said, raising his voice. "It will do no good."

"Oh, Daniel," his mother said.

Now he was mad. "What is this?" he said, the tears starting to flow. "If I'm supposed to have done something, I have a right to know what it is. What did I do?"

"Plagiarism," Mr. Estes thundered. "As if you didn't know!"

"I don't even know what that means." Daniel said. "What are you talking about?"

"It's like stealing," the principal said. "Only it's stealing ideas — stealing another person's work."

"I've never done that in my life," Daniel said, looking to his mother for support. But she was staring at the floor. He had never felt so alone, or so guilty.

But he still didn't know what Mr. Estes was talking about. And he said so.

"What do you call this, then?" Mr. Estes

asked, as he handed Daniel what appeared to be a report. Daniel's hands shook as he looked through it. It was typed, and the title was "A Solar-Powered Community."

"I've never seen this before," he said.

Mr. Estes slammed his hand down on the desk. "Oh, come now!" he said.

"I haven't! What is it?"

"Look closely. Do you recognize it?"

"Well, it's just like my report, only it's typed. Who did this? Whose is it?"

"You know very well whose it is, young man," Mr. Estes said.

"I don't! You believe me, don't you, Mom?"

But his mother wasn't looking at him.

9

The
Accusation

For an instant Daniel wondered if he were having a nightmare. But this was all too real. He was crying. His mother was crying and wouldn't look at him. His teacher looked so disappointed. And Mr. Estes was accusing him of something!

The principal shook his head sadly. "The name has been removed from this old science theme, Mr. Bradford," he said, calming down. "But you know whose it is, because it is the one you copied for your report."

"I didn't!"

"You did! But let me finish. You copied it even to the sketches for your model community. Over the lunch hour I visited Mrs. Quarry's classroom, and I was amazed to find an exact replica of the drawing in this report — a model commu-

"Why did you copy this?"

nity that you built and represented as your own work."

"It *was* my own work."

"You may have built it, Mr. Bradford, but it was not your original idea."

"It *was*."

Mr. Estes stood again. "I must tell you, young man, it greatly angers me when you talk back to me."

"But I — "

"I want you to stop it, and I want you to stop denying that you copied this project. It's very clear that this original is eight years old. It was done by a former student here, but he was not satisfied with it. He put it back in his files and tried something else. That something won him the science project prize and a ribbon in the state competition.

"So, you see, Mr. Bradford, your stolen idea may have been very impressive at first, and you did an outstanding job of copying, but you copied too closely. You gave yourself away."

Daniel just sat shaking his head. He was afraid to defend himself again, because he didn't want to anger the principal anymore. It was obvious they didn't believe him, and now he wasn't sure what to think himself.

Just from what Mr. Estes had said, he knew

that the paper belonged to Ken Majors. He was the only student to ever win a ribbon in state competition. Every time Mr. Estes called him "Mr. Bradford," Daniel thought of his father and wished he were here. He knew his dad would believe him.

They sat in silence for a moment, then Daniel tried again. "I never even knew Ken Majors, you know. I mean, I know who he is, but I have never even talked to him. He is a lot older than I am, and he's off at college."

"So, you're admitting that you copied one of his old papers?" Mrs. Quarry asked. The principal sat down and leaned back in his chair.

"No, I am not."

Mr. Estes pounded the desk again. "Then how did you know whose paper this was? I covered the name and the date, and I said nothing about it!"

"From what you said about him! I know Scotty, and I've seen Ken's picture in the trophy case. I know all about him."

"Indeed, you do!"

"But I never copied anything by him."

"Mr. Bradford, your mother has seen both your report and Ken Majors' report. She has seen for herself that they are almost identical. She hasn't looked at your model since you brought it to school, but she agrees that the drawing in Ken Majors' report looks just like what you built in your basement. She also says that you did all the work yourself."

"Of course, I did. That was the rule."

"Don't talk to me about the rules after what you've done, young man. You built this on your own so you could copy it correctly."

Daniel wanted to scream. He was innocent! How could he make them believe him? He just sat shaking his head and staring straight into Mr. Estes' eyes. Maybe the old man would wonder how he could look right at him if he were guilty.

But the principal just stared right back at Daniel. "There is a solution to this matter, at least from my viewpoint," he said. "I want you to admit you did it, accept a failing grade for your project, dismantle it, and admit your mistake to your class."

Daniel was stunned. He wanted out of this situation so badly that he was almost tempted to do it. Why did he feel guilty? It was almost as if he had done everything the principal said he had.

"Who says I did this?" he asked.

"Does it matter?"

"Of course. Don't I have a right to know?"

"You probably already know."

Daniel nodded. It had to be Scotty. But how did he do it? How did he make it look so real? "Where did you get that paper? From Scotty?"

The principal nodded.

"Then how was I supposed to copy it?"

"You had your own copy."

"I did not! How can you say that?"

The principal nodded to Mrs. Quarry. She held up a photocopy of the original. "I found this in your desk this morning," she said.

"In my desk?"

Finally, Mrs. Bradford spoke. "May I take my son home?" she asked.

"If he'll come back tomorrow and do what I've outlined," Mr. Estes said.

"I believe he will," she said, "but he needs to make things right at home, too. He has other people to apologize to."

"Who?" Daniel demanded.

"Don't make things worse, Honey," his mother said.

"I want to know who you think I have to apologize to!" he shouted.

Mrs. Bradford spoke softly. "I don't want these people to think that we allow you to speak to your parents this way, Daniel," she said.

"Is that all you care about? What they think?

You don't care that I'm being accused of something I didn't do? I want to know whom you want me to admit this to when I didn't do it!"

"To God, for one," she said. "And then to everyone in your family that you misled. When you have everyone's forgiveness, you'll be able to come back here and make things right."

"I won't do it!" he said.

"You may take him home," the principal said. "I can't get through to him. I hope you can."

"My husband will be home. I'm sure we can handle it."

"Dad already knows about this?"

She nodded, and Daniel burst into tears. "Now I'll never have a chance with him. He probably already thinks I'm guilty!"

"Is there anything you need from your desk?" his mother asked as they walked toward the car. He shook his head. He never wanted to show his face in that classroom again.

"What are you going to tell your little sister?" Mrs. Bradford said in the car.

"You mean I get to talk to her before you do?" he asked angrily.

She looked very sad, but she nodded. "I'd almost rather she didn't know about this."

"Well, I'm going to tell her," he said. "For once someone's going to get my side of it first."

"What is your side of it, Daniel?"

"Oh, you're finally interested in that? My side is that I didn't do it. I didn't copy anything, and I never saw that other report before. If I did, I don't remember it."

"You mean you might have seen it before and it somehow stayed in your mind — then came out as your own thoughts?" she suggested.

"Is that possible?" he asked.

"Is that your story?"

"No! I just want to know if it's possible."

"Not really. It wouldn't have come back to you word for word. Daniel, why did you do it?"

He climbed over the seat into the back and buried his head in his hands, crying all the way home.

"God will forgive you, Daniel," his mother said. "And we will, too. But you must tell the truth."

"I don't want to talk about it," he said. He wanted to talk to Yolanda. And he wanted to talk to his dad. If they didn't believe him, he wanted to die.

10

"Come Clean, Dan"

Daniel started up to his room as soon as they got home. He wanted to slam his door and lock it, and then pray that his mother would believe him.

But she called after him as he bounded up the stairs. "Stay down here, Daniel," she said. "We are going to talk about this right now!"

"I don't want to talk about it until Dad gets back!" he said.

"He's not coming home for five days, Daniel, unless I have to call him back here to talk some sense into you."

Daniel plopped down on the couch. "He won't be able to make me admit I did it," he said. "No one will, ever."

His mother sat across from him in an over-stuffed chair. "Daniel, you know I'd rather have you admit what you did and take your punishment, because if you keep lying about it your punishment will have to be more severe."

He stared at her. "Why won't you believe me, Mom? If I can't convince you, then I might as well admit something I didn't do and get it over with."

"I don't want you to admit it until you're willing to say you were wrong, and that you'll go back to school and apologize to the class."

He sat silently.

"You can think about it for awhile," his mother said.

"I'm not thinking about it," he said. "I didn't do it, and I won't be saying that I did, even if you ground me for a year."

She acted as if she hadn't heard him. "And when you get to the place where you're ready to ask forgiveness, I want you to ask God's forgiveness, too."

Daniel smiled, even in his misery.

"Something funny about this?" she said.

"Yeah. God's the only one who knows I'm innocent."

"That's not funny, Daniel. Now you may go to your room."

Daniel cried long and hard as he lay on his bed. And he did pray about his problem. Mostly he prayed that someone would believe him — that he would be so convincing that everyone would *have* to believe him.

A weak knock on the door made him jump. "Who is it?"

"Yolanda."

"Come in, Yo-Yo."

"Mom said you got in trouble today, and that you could tell me about it if you wanted to."

Daniel told her the whole story.

"Well, where did that other report come from then, Daniel?" she asked.

"You don't believe me either," Daniel muttered.

"Of course I do. I just want to help you prove it."

"How should I know where the typed report came from? Scotty has to be behind it — his dad has an electric typewriter. The report even had a sketch of my project in it."

"Well?"

"I know I never saw it before. That's all."

That night at dinner Jim and Maryann tried to add their ideas. Daniel was angry that his mother had told them all about it herself. From what they were saying, it was clear that they didn't believe him either. He didn't want to eat anything.

"Dan," Jim said, "if you aren't guilty, you shouldn't act guilty."

"How would you act if no one believed you?" Daniel demanded.

"I believe you!" Yolanda piped up.

"I don't think I do," Maryann said.

Daniel hung his head. "Mom, you see what happens when *you* tell the story? Nobody believes me. When I got to tell it from the beginning myself, Yolanda believed me. You'd better let me talk to Dad before you do."

Jim and Maryann looked at each other and then at their mother. "Too late," she said. "I talked with him about half an hour ago."

"And what did he say?"

"He said he'd come home and deal with it if necessary."

Daniel stood up. His face was red and tears were streaming down his cheeks. "What's that supposed to mean?"

His mother didn't say anything. "Just come clean, Dan," Jim said. "Tell the kids at school what you did and get it over with. Life will be a lot easier for you."

Daniel nearly screamed. "What do you know? You think I did it, and you're wrong! So don't be tellin' *me* how to handle it!"

Jim held up both hands as if to surrender. "All right, Kid. I just hope I'm not here when Dad gets home tomorrow."

Daniel stormed up to his room, followed by Yolanda. "Leave me alone!" he yelled.

"I believe you, Daniel."

"Yeah, but that's just because I told you my side first. If Mom had told you, you'd have believed her."

"No, I wouldn't. Because I know you, and you never lie."

"I lied two years ago and had to admit it. That's why Mom doesn't believe me now — and Dad won't either. And if I can't convince them, I'm leaving here."

"What do you mean you're leaving here?" Yolanda said. "Where will you go?"

"To Grandpa Bradford. He's lonely, so he'll be glad to have me. Anyway, he'll believe me if I can get to him before Mom does."

"Can I come with you?"

"Sure, if you want to."

"I'm not sure," she said.

"Then don't."

"I mean, I just got into this family this summer, and I like it here."

"Well, I used to. But I can't stay where nobody trusts me."

Yolanda looked sad. "You're the one I like most, so I'll go with you. We'll come back though, won't we?"

"When people believe me, I'll come back."

So they made their plans. If Daniel's father couldn't be convinced the next night, Daniel wanted to leave around two in the morning.

"Are you sure Dad is coming home tomorrow?" Yolanda asked.

"You bet."

"How do you know?"

"You heard Mom. She said if I didn't admit it, he'd come home and handle it."

"What does that mean?"

"Oh, he has his ways of making me do what I should, or what he wants."

"But you said he couldn't make you admit it."

"He can't, but he'll try."

"But how can you be sure he'll come home tomorrow when he's not supposed to be back until Friday?"

"You'll see."

Daniel spent the rest of the evening talking first to Maryann and then to Jim. He didn't seem to be getting anywhere, but Jim asked an awful lot of questions about his project and the paper.

"You gonna do what you have to do at school tomorrow?" Jim asked him.

Daniel shrugged. "I don't know. What do I have to do?"

"You know exactly what you have to do. The right thing."

"The right thing? Yeah, I'll do the right thing."

Just before bedtime, Mrs. Bradford knocked on Daniel's door. "Dan," she said, "have you prayed about this?"

"Yes," he said, nodding and looking as relieved as possible.

"That's good. I'm proud of you. And happy for you. Do you feel better about it now?"

"A little."

"I knew you would." She paused and said, "Jim thinks you're going to do the right thing in school tomorrow."

"I sure am."

11
Daniel
Does
Right
Thing

Many of the students in Daniel's class acted awkward around him the next morning. He knew they must have been talking about him and his problem.

He stared at Scotty Majors several times, but Scotty wouldn't look at him.

Just before the class began, Mrs. Quarry leaned over his desk. "I talked with your mother this morning," she said. "She tells me that you're here today because you promised to do the right thing."

Daniel nodded.

"I'm proud of you, Daniel, and I want you to know that I forgive you. The class will forgive you, too — even Scott Majors' older brother will forgive you. It will be difficult for you, and you'll probably never forget this day as long as you live, but it takes a real man to do this."

Daniel didn't say anything. He thought about nodding again, but he decided against that, too.

"When would you like to speak to the class?"

"As soon as possible," he said. "I'd kinda like to get it over with."

She smiled. "I know what you mean."

After the bell rang and Mrs. Quarry took the roll and led the class in the pledge to the flag, she said, "We're going to begin today by having Daniel Bradford share with the class again for just a few minutes. Daniel?"

Daniel walked slowly to the front. Carefully he took the blanket off his project again. He sneaked a glance at Mrs. Quarry, and he noticed that she looked puzzled.

"You remember what I showed you yesterday," Daniel began, his voice shaky. "I, uh, told my mom and Mrs. Quarry that I would do the right thing about it. So I just want to say that this project, this whole thing here, everything from the plywood to all the pieces, I built myself."

"It was my own idea. I thought it up myself. I drew it up, I found all the pieces, and I put it together myself. I didn't copy anything or anyone."

Mrs. Quarry stood up and sternly said,

Come with me!

"Daniel!" But he kept talking and ignored her.

"My paper, the one I memorized and then turned in, was my own work, not stolen or copied."

By now Mrs. Quarry was walking toward him.

"And I don't care what anybody says. I did my own work! Whoever made that phony copy is the liar and the cheater."

"Come with me, young man," Mrs. Quarry said. She gripped Daniel's arm so hard that he wrenched away, causing her to grab him again, even harder.

She took him to Mr. Estes office where he waited until his mother came for him.

This time his mother was more than hurt and disappointed. She was angry.

She slammed her car door and said nothing to him all the way home. That was fine with Daniel. "Did you call Dad yet?" he asked, almost too easily.

She nodded, as if expecting that would scare him. It didn't. It was just what he wanted. He wanted a chance to tell Dad his story.

When they entered the house, his mother spoke for the first time. "You lied to me," she said. He was shocked. "You said you would do the right thing today. You told Jim the same thing."

"I did the right thing, Mom," Daniel said, calmer now than ever. He had given up on her, and his older brother and sister, and his teacher and the principal. There was no sense getting upset about it.

He would try to convince his dad, and, if that didn't work, he and Yolanda were going to Grandpa Bradford's.

Daniel was still in his room when his mother and brother returned from the airport with his dad that evening. Maryann had stayed with Daniel and Yolanda, but she fell asleep on the couch while they planned their two o'clock escape. "Just in case Dad doesn't believe me," Daniel had said.

Yolanda had nodded.

When Bob Bradford entered Daniel's room, he looked tired and sad. "There's nothing more important to me in the world than my family, Dan," he said. "I never gave a second thought to staying in Florida until Friday, knowing that I was needed here."

"I need you, all right," Daniel said. "I need you to believe me."

"I'm listening."

His father heard the whole story, and even pulled some paper from his pocket and took some notes. Daniel couldn't figure that out. Maybe he was going to check up on Daniel's story or something.

When Daniel had finished, he was crying again. He hadn't wanted to cry, because he was afraid it made him look guilty. But halfway through his story he had realized how sick and disappointed he was that only Yolanda believed him.

And he was desperate! What if his dad didn't believe him either? He didn't really want to leave, to run away from his great family. He'd had such good times, and he loved them all so much. And now he had a sister closer to his age.

Things should have been perfect! Why did it have to happen? Who was doing it to him and why? He looked deep into his father eyes, silently praying that he would believe him.

His dad sat looking at him for a long time. Daniel hoped he would clap him on the back, or hug him, or something, but he didn't. He just stood, turned his back to Daniel, and walked to the window.

He looked outside for a long time. "Thanks for telling me your story, Daniel," he said. "I appreciate it."

Daniel didn't know what to say. He wanted to just come right out and ask his dad if he believed him, but he was afraid of the answer. His dad sounded real sad, and Daniel couldn't tell what that meant.

Daniel wondered if he should tell his dad how frustrated he was that no one believed him, or how he thought the phony copy of his report was made, or who he thought did it and why.

"I owe it to you to be very frank with you," Mr. Bradford said, finally turning around and facing him. Daniel still wished he'd come closer. "This reminds me an awful lot of the time you lied to us about something that belonged to Jim. In fact, it reminds me too much. You were very earnest and convincing then, too, and I almost believed you, as I almost believe you now."

"But you don't," Daniel said, tears coming again.

"No, I don't."

The words cut through Daniel like a knife. His last hope was gone. He knew that no matter what else his dad said, he didn't believe him. Dad would never believe him unless Daniel could prove it, and he didn't know where to start.

He would be leaving in a few hours with Yolanda, and probably get in the biggest trouble of his life, but he didn't care anymore. He had to get out of there. He had to go where someone believed his side of the story.

104

"I love you, Daniel, and I know you must be sick about this."

"I'm sick about nobody believing me, Dad!"

But his dad ignored him.

"I'm going to stay home from work, and you're going to stay home from school, until this is settled one way or the other, Son. Understand?"

Daniel nodded. He understood all right. The truth was that nobody believed a kid. Why did they believe Scotty Majors? He must have been the one who showed Mrs. Quarry the so-called original report.

Life wasn't fair. His dad talked some more about honesty and character and reputation and family trust, but Daniel's mind was on his trip. What if it rained? What should he take? Would Yolanda be ready?

"What I want you to do is to pray about this a lot, and think about it a lot, Daniel. Then in the morning, when you get up — early enough to go to school if you're ready to get this settled — or later if you still want to talk about it — I'll be here, waiting to talk to you. Fair enough?"

Daniel nodded.

"I know you'll make the right decision, Dan. And, when you do, the punishment will be fair. The longer this goes on, the more serious it will have to be. You're too big and too old for spanking, but we'll work something out."

That was when Daniel knew there would be no turning back. His father had not said anything about what would happen if it was proved that Daniel was innocent. That wasn't part of the plan.

Everyone was convinced he was guilty, and when he was ready to admit it, he could take his punishment and be done with it.

But he would never be ready for that.

12

Caught!

Several hours after the talk with his dad, Daniel woke up on a wide seat of the passenger train heading for Grandpa Bradford's.

The bright morning sunlight made him squint. He checked all around him and found that everything was still in place. He had some money left, but not much.

He looked on the floor beneath him to see if he had dropped his ticket. It was not there, so he knew the conductor must have taken it from him while he slept.

He put his foot under him so he could push up and look back at Yolanda. But his leg hurt so much that he could hardly move it. He leaned around to see her. She was sound asleep, breathing heavily and deeply like a baby.

He felt bad about dragging her into all this, but he just had to have someone with him who believed him. He wondered if she still did, after all the lies he had told.

He tried to change positions, but his leg was so sore that it made him cry out. That woke Yolanda. She sat up, rubbed her eyes and stretched. She tried to see out the window but was blinded by the sun.

"Where are we, Daniel?" she asked. "I'm hungry."

"Almost there," he said. "We'll buy something at the station."

"How's your leg?"

"Fine."

"Let me see."

"Nah."

"Let me see, Daniel!"

He knew she would wish she hadn't asked. He pulled the leg of his pants up and found the sock stuck to his leg. It hurt so much to pull it away from the wound, but he didn't have any choice. He would have to wash his leg and put a clean sock over the cut.

He almost cried as he pulled the sock off. When he hobbled to the washroom, it was so painful that he wondered if he could get in a bus or taxi. He would need to do that to get to his grandfather's once they got into the station.

What he saw in the washroom scared him. His leg was swollen and discolored. He didn't know much about disease and infection, but he knew he would have to get to a doctor soon. The faster they got to Grandpa's the better.

He didn't want to worry Yolanda, but he decided that if he saw a wheelchair in the station he would ask for it. He'd seen old people and crippled people use them. "You can push me in it, Yo-Yo," he said. "I can carry our bags in my lap. If anyone's looking for us, they won't be looking for a wheelchair. It'll be a good disguise."

"Then why don't *you* push *me* in the chair?" she asked.

"Because I've got the bad leg."

"Then it *does* hurt."

"A little."

As the train began to slow down gradually, the conductor came by and said, "You kids better find your mom now."

Daniel nodded, and they lugged their bags through to the next car, the opposite direction from where the conductor was going.

When they got off the train, Daniel winced from the pain in his leg. He noticed two policemen at the end of the platform. In a way he almost hoped they were looking for him and Yolanda. But then his sense of desperation took over.

He had to keep going — he had to get to Grandpa's. He couldn't give up until his name was cleared. He wasn't sure yet how Grandpa could help, but maybe just knowing they had taken so much trouble to come all this way would convince him that Daniel was telling the truth.

Daniel limped past the line where the conductor was helping people down the steps. He saw an old woman in a wheelchair being pushed toward the train. "C'mon, Yolanda," he called, walking behind them. "When he helps her out of the chair, we'll ask him for it."

But when the porter helped the lady out of the chair, and gave her her blanket and purse, Daniel lost his nerve to ask. He just sat in the chair and signaled Yolanda to push.

He had taken Yolanda by surprise. The porter was turning around and reaching for the chair, so she dropped her bag into Daniel's lap and tried to get him rolling.

He hunched and lurched back and forth to help, but she was not big or strong, and he was heavier than she was. The chair wasn't exactly light either. "C'mon, push!" he said.

Push!!!

"I'm trying."

Finally they were moving, but Daniel sensed they were not going straight. He slouched down in the chair to hide behind the bags. As he peeked out, he saw them angling for the edge of the platform.

They were already over the yellow line and heading for the hissing engine. "How do you steer this thing?" Yolanda called.

"Just yank it!" he yelped.

So she yanked it. Now they were on one wheel, then back down onto the two big ones, and then onto the two little ones in front. One of them was wobbling and spinning as they moved toward a crowd of people heading into the terminal.

"Slow down, Yo-Yo!" She couldn't hear him, so he hollered at the crowd. "Watch out! Clear the way!" Some turned to scowl at him before they realized how fast he was coming. "Emergency!" he screamed, and people ran for cover.

He was laughing so hard he couldn't catch his breath. Then he saw they were edging through a narrow doorway and toward some steps. He didn't want to be anywhere near a stairway with Yolanda piloting the chair.

"Okay, I'll walk from here," he said. But she was still running. He turned around. "Stop,

Yo-Yo!" The stairs were now just twenty feet away, and she was running toward them at full speed.

She dug in her heels, but, rather than stopping the chair, it only slowed it ever so slightly before she lost her grip. Daniel was still looking back as Yolanda stopped to watch the chair roll toward the stairs.

Her eyes grew big, and Daniel didn't want to look. He gripped a bag in each hand and just rolled out the front and off to the side of the chair. He knocked his head on the floor, but he fell clear of the chair as it rattled down the stairs.

A young man on the stairs jumped out of the way, and, as far as Daniel could tell, no one was hurt. His head ached and his leg felt as if it were about to explode. He sensed people gathering around him, so he hobbled over to Yolanda and dragged her out to a taxi. They jumped into the back seat.

"Where to, kids?"

"Route 11 past the combine — to the Bradford place. You know it?"

"Sure. You got money?"

Daniel waved a few bills at him.

"How long will this take, Daniel?" Yolanda said. "I'm starving. I don't know when I've been so hungry."

"About twenty minutes. Can you wait till we get there?"

"No."

"Stop for some doughnuts, please," Daniel said. "After we get on the highway."

"Whatever you say, Kid," the driver said, smiling into the rearview mirror. "You know there's nobody at the Bradford place."

"What do you mean?"

"The old man is the only one who lives there now."

"I know, he's my grandpa."

"Well, you grandpa's gone on vacation, Sonny. Been gone about four days, I think. Won't be back for a coupla weeks. I'm not sure where he went."

"How do you know that?" Yolanda asked.

"I'm from out that way, Honey. Everybody knows everybody. We watch out for the old man."

"I knew that," Daniel said quickly. He had to think hard about what to say next. "Grandpa said I could play in the barn while he was gone. I know where he keeps the key to the house, too."

"You sure?" the driver said.

"'Course."

"I don't know if I should leave you out there alone."

114

"We won't be staying long. We'll be going back tonight. And for the short time we'll be here, there isn't a whole lot that can happen to us."

All the while, Daniel was thinking to himself that he hoped he was right.

13

Ask
for
Forgiveness

Stuffed to the gills on glazed, powdered, and jellied doughnuts, Daniel and Yolanda settled back for the ride to Grandpa Bradford's farm.

Daniel was nearly sick, wondering what they were going to do if Grandpa really wasn't there. He knew he needed help for his leg, but he didn't want to ask the cab driver.

As they pulled around the wide curve and into the long driveway of Grandpa's place, however, two squad cars pulled out from the side of the road and followed them.

There was no need for lights or sirens. There was no other way out except back the way they had come. "What's this now?" the driver asked, staring in his rearview mirror.

Daniel looked back and immediately slipped

to the floor, pulling little Yolanda down with him. "You haven't seen us," Daniel said. "Just tell 'em you're lost or something!"

"I can't do that. Forget it."

"Please!"

By now the cab driver had stopped and was rolling down his window. The police officer asked to see his license and registration, then asked who he had in the car. The driver might have tried to protect the kids, except the policeman could see them on the floor.

Rather than waiting for an answer, he just opened the back door and peered in. "Your name wouldn't happen to be Yolanda Bradford, would it?" he said. She nodded. "And you must be Daniel."

"Daniel's hurt," Yolanda said quickly.

"Shh!" Daniel said.

"It's all right, Daniel," the policeman said. "We heard you were limping, and even had a short ride in a wheelchair. Let's have a look at your leg."

"You two got farther than your parents thought you might," the policeman said as Daniel waited in a medical clinic. "When your bike was found out near the highway, they had quite a scare."

"How'd they know where to find us?" Daniel asked.

"Oh, I don't think it was that hard to figure out. Where else were you going to go?"

"I thought about California."

"That's a long way from here," the policeman said, smiling.

"That's where I'm going next," Daniel said, still scowling.

"You still upset at your parents?"

Daniel nodded.

"It was a pretty dangerous thing you did, bringing your little sister with you. You think this is going to make your parents believe you?"

"I was hoping my grandfather would."

"I believe you."

Daniel was surprised. What was the policeman trying to say? He didn't know anything about what had happened except what he had heard — probably by telephone — from Daniel's parents. "How would you know if I was telling the truth or not?"

"I think your trip proves it. This isn't a guilty person's trip. This is an innocent person's trip."

Daniel wanted to cry. "Will you tell that to my parents?"

"I already have."

"Do they believe you?"

"I don't know. I think your mother does. Mostly they were just worried about you two.

You're going to owe them a big apology for that."

Daniel didn't know what to say. He thought he was owed some big apologies, too. "Were they just afraid, or do you think this convinced them?"

"They'll have to tell you that themselves. They'll be here in a couple of hours."

"Am I in trouble?"

"Oh, I think maybe a little. Your leg is going to take some work."

"I know. But I'm more worried about what Mom and Dad think."

"I would be, too. Your whole class in school is wondering where you are."

"They are?"

"Yes. Everyone has been talking about your disappearance. One of the first places the police in your town looked was at your school. Then, when your bike was found and people in the train stations remembered seeing you, we were called to stake out your grandfather's house."

"Stake out?"

"Watch it to see if you showed up."

"Oh."

Daniel felt tired and a little relieved, but he was scared about a doctor working on his leg.

"Is there a girl in your class named Amy?" the policeman asked.

"Yes! Amy Noble. What about her?"

"Well, she felt so bad when she heard you were missing that she admitted she had damaged your project. Your science project or something."

"She did? My solar community?"

"I guess. She pulled a wire and bent something over when she was the only one in the room. She was afraid that made you mad and that was why you ran away."

"But that wasn't it at all! I thought that was done by the same guy who tried to get me in trouble. Did she admit anything else?"

"Not that I know of."

A couple of hours later, Daniel was trying to rest on a cot at the police station. He was full of medicine and had a tight bandage covering seven stitches in his leg. It was still throbbing.

He began to cry as soon as he heard his parents' voices. "I'm sorry, Mom," he said, as she ran to him and hugged him. Dad lifted Yolanda high in the air and squeezed her tight.

"That's not important right now," his mother said. "We're just glad God answered our prayers and protected you."

"I know you'll have to yell at me for all the

It really hurts.

things I did," he said, "but that's all right too."

"Yes, we will," his dad said. "You know better."

"But I had to do something, Dad! No one believed me, and I was innocent!"

"I know," his mother said. "I believe you now." But his dad was silent.

"Then it was worth it," Daniel said.

"No, it wasn't!" Mr. Bradford said. "Nothing was worth this!"

He was called to the phone.

"Doesn't Dad believe me, Mom?"

"I think he does, Daniel, but that doesn't make it right. You ran off and scared us to death."

"I know, but —"

"Let's not talk about it now. We'll have to hash it all out later."

"That's what I'm afraid of."

Mr. Bradford returned, looking deep in thought. "That was Jim," he said. "You know what he asked me? He asked me if the damage to your project was done before or after we set it up in your class. I guess he hadn't heard about Amy's confession."

"What about it, Dad?"

"Well, Jim went to the school and looked at the report you were supposed to have copied. The sketch of the project shows both mistakes in it. The wire was sticking up, and the one solar reactor plate is bent over like yours was."

"I don't get it," Daniel said.

"Neither do I," his mother said.

"It means that the sketch in the phony report was done not only after we set up the project, but also after Amy pulled the wire and bent the plate. Jim's calling Scotty Majors' brother Ken at his college to see if he ever did a report or project like that."

"And if he didn't?"

"Then Scotty is in big trouble."

"And I'm innocent."

"You're already innocent, Daniel," Mr. Bradford said. "The sketch proved that. Now we just have to find out who did it and why. Can Scotty type?"

"Sure!" Daniel said. "He's slow, but he's pretty good."

"I think Scotty did it, and for the same reason Amy did what she did," Mrs. Bradford said. "Jealousy. It was obvious to them when they saw the project that it was going to win."

On the way home, Mr. and Mrs. Bradford each took a long time to tell Daniel that they knew they'd been wrong about him and that they were sorry they didn't trust him. "We're still going to have to deal with this running off," his dad said, "but we know we're partly to blame for that.

You'll never do anything like this again, will you Daniel?"

"Yes! And soon!"

His dad jerked around and stared at him.

"I have to make this same trip again, as soon as I can, Dad. Yo-Yo needs to meet Grandpa and I owe apologies. I lied to a lot of people, and I need their forgiveness. I need God's forgiveness too."

"Yeah," Yolanda said. "He lied to a lot of people along the way!"

"Fair enough," his father said. "When your leg is better, and your project wins first place, we'll all go with you."

Two weeks later, Daniel's leg was better.

A blue ribbon hung inside his bedroom door.

And his father kept his promise.

A brand new series!

The Jennifer Books

By Jane Sorensen

Jennifer Green talks to God. Everyday. Often, several times a day. In her first book, **It's Me, Jennifer,** she's twelve years old when she meets God by going to Sunday school for the first time. There she learns that God is her friend and she begins to tell Him about the important things in her life. Things like her first high-school basketball game, her first two-piece swimsuit, her first game of tennis with a boy (was that a *date*, Lord?), and her exciting, but disappointing Christmas.

Just before the end of seventh grade, she finds out that **It's Your Move, Jennifer,** because her dad has been promoted and the whole family will be moving to Philadelphia. What's it like to leave the only home, school, and friends you've ever known? Find out as Jennifer does and as she shares her thoughts with God.

In **Jennifer's New Life,** Jennifer adjusts to a new city, new school, new friends, and her first church retreat. The speakers at the retreat help her to understand that God wants to be more than just her friend, and she becomes a Christian. Now she faces a new set of problems: What will the kids at school think? What will her parents and younger brothers think? The retreat leader said she would share Christ with at least one other person – how can she do *that*? Together with God, Jennifer finds the answers.

Finally, in **Jennifer Says Good-bye,** Jennifer experiences some very grown-up emotions. She begins to understand how deeply she can love another family member, and how very much it hurts when that person dies. But through the sorrow that she shares with her family, something wonderful begins to happen and Jennifer learns that kids can be a great help to their parents.

If you ever have to deal with emotions like fear, loneliness, excitement, wanting to belong, disappointment, learning to love, or sorrow, you'll enjoy reading **The Jennifer Books.**

How lucky can some kids get?

It seems like Eric and Alison, the Thorne twins, are always running into adventure. The most ordinary things become unusual when they are involved.

The Great UFO Chase   In this seventeenth book of the series, a brainy student visits the Thornes, and brings with him a lot more than his books! Is it purely coincidental that residents of Ivy, Illinois, begin sighting UFO's just after this stranger arrives? What kind of transmission is disturbing the radio-station signals, and why are Air Force officials interested in the Thornes' houseguest? Eric asks these questions and more before he finally finds the answers to *The Great UFO Chase*.

The Olympic Plot   Alison unknowingly becomes a threat to the lives of the President and Vice President of the United States. She knows only that she is not in complete control of her actions, and that she forgets segments of time. How can she help Eric uncover the plot when neither of them is sure there *is* a plot? Their visit to Olympic Village becomes a nightmare of kidnappings, fake athletes, and sickness, while the time for murder draws closer and closer.

Secret of Pirates' Cave   When a classmate of Eric's presents an exciting report of how pirates once raided his ancestors, Eric repeats the story at home. He and Alison are thrilled to discover that their own ancestors were on the same ship, and were raided by the same pirate. Mr. Thorne shows them half of a map that supposedly leads to the families' treasure, and the search is on!

Before the treasure can be recovered, the kids must deal with secret tunnels, a "monster cave," and a ghost who doesn't want the past disturbed!

If you like adventure stories, be sure to read these and other books in the Thorne Twin series.